A
GIRL'S
BEST
FRIEND

Other Apple Paperbacks by
HARRIET MAY SAVITZ:

The Cats Nobody Wanted

Swimmer

The Bullies and Me

A GIRL'S BEST FRIEND

HARRIET·MAY·SAVITZ

AN
APPLE
PAPERBACK

SCHOLASTIC INC.
New York Toronto London Auckland Sydney

ISBN 0-590-45708-X

12 11 10 9 8 7 6 5 4 3 2 1   5 6 7 8 9/9 0/0

Printed in the U.S.A.   40

First Scholastic printing, December 1995

To George Blackstock,
who knows everything there is
to know about repairing bicycles;
to Serena Cucco,
who enjoys riding them;
and to Barbara Cheadle,
editor of Future Reflections, *published by the*
National Federation of the Blind, Inc.
Thank you, Barbara,
for opening my eyes.

1

Laurie heard Jessie's soft moan as she jumped to the floor from the bed. Jessie repeated the painful complaint as she settled on the floor.

"Poor dog, Jessie. You don't feel good this afternoon, do you?" She tried to soothe the dog as she bent down and stroked her long ears, which were spotted by black and white circles of fur. Jessie moved from beneath her touch as if even the gentle stroking caused her pain.

"Come on, Jessie," Laurie coaxed, motioning her forward. "You've got to feel better. I know you can do it. Today's your birthday."

The dog's tail thumped a loving greeting as she nestled in Laurie's lap.

"Maybe it's just because it's raining out. Don't you hear it on the windows? It rained all night and it's been raining all day, Jessie. Mom says the arthritis in her fingers gets worse when it rains. And her big toe always hurts just like a toothache. Maybe the same thing happens to you."

Laurie always had discussions with Jessie, especially in the afternoon when she got back from school. But today she couldn't tell her pet everything that was in her heart. And she certainly didn't feel like telling Jessie about the big decision, the one her parents said had to be made soon, the one that Laurie refused to talk about whenever they wanted to discuss it.

But she could tell her about Josephine. "You wouldn't like her either," Laurie whispered as she brushed Jessie's fine coat, once thick, but lately thinning with old age. "I never knew anyone like her in the old school, Jessie. She's just everywhere I go and she always has something nasty to say. Like today, know what she said? 'Can't you see where you're going?' I told her, 'Of course, I know where I'm going. I'm blind, not stupid.' But Jessie, how could I get to where I was going if she was standing right in front of me and wouldn't move? I sure wish she went to another school."

Laurie waited for Jessie to jump up as she usually did on her good days and fetch her ball. But today she showed no interest in playing the game or in searching for her favorite treasure, socks.

"Where're my socks?" Laurie's dad yelled every morning, at least every morning during Jessie's younger years. Jessie loved collecting socks more than eating pretzels that she begged for, or pistachio nuts that she shelled and ate the insides.

Jessie waited for those socks to be dropped each morning and each night. Sometimes Laurie's father would put them in the hamper, but it was as if Jessie knew the nights he was too tired or forgetful and then they would be there stuffed in his shoes. Jessie always knew when to strike.

She'd bury those socks under something, or behind something, or inside her sleeping basket in the living room. On Jessie's devilish days, she would chew them up until there was just a hole where the toe should have been. Laurie almost wished she would do that now, bury or chew up socks, bark her beagle howl at the window, get into some kind of trouble instead of just lying there on the floor, listless. Jessie was only silent and still when she didn't feel well.

"I know, girl, that you're suffering. Mom's arthritis just bothers her fingers, but she can go to work anyway. But on your bad days, you don't even feel like walking, do you, old dog?"

The words slipped out, the words she hated to hear her father say. "Don't call her 'old dog,' " she'd protest whenever she heard it. And now she was saying it, too. She was beginning to sound like her parents.

"It's a shame for that old dog," her mother and father kept telling her on Jessie's bad days, as if they thought she could do something about it. Laurie knew what they wanted to do. But she wouldn't let them even talk about it.

"You want to go out, girl?" Laurie asked.

Jessie rubbed against her legs to tell her she was ready to go in the backyard, sniff around the bushes, and maybe even find an old bone she had buried there. Laurie was usually the first one home after school, now that her sister, Katherine, had left for college. Jessie was all hers, and so was Katherine's larger room. Laurie had moved into it with her sister's permission.

"Come on, girl." Laurie opened the back door to let Jessie outside. They had fenced in the backyard just for her.

On the good days, Jessie would playfully jump up on Laurie's legs and stretch her body so that she could be kissed on the nose before she went into the backyard. Though she didn't mean to do it, her nails would scratch on the way down. Laurie wouldn't have minded that today. She wouldn't have minded the scratches or anything else that Jessie usually did when she felt frisky. Like stealing food off the table. Nobody could leave a sandwich unguarded if Jessie was around. Even the teacher at the training school they had sent her to as a puppy admitted defeat.

"She's like a human vacuum cleaner," the teacher said. "That beagle just sucks up food wherever it is."

Only a few minutes had passed when Jessie barked her signal to come in. Laurie opened the back door, then went to the large cookie jar that

4

was on the table right next to it. Instead of cookies, Jessie's Milk-Bones were kept in the round glass jar. Jessie usually expected one in the morning when she went out and one in the afternoon when Laurie returned from school.

She felt Jessie's thank-you in her warm mouth as it nuzzled her hand and the bone in it. "You're not giving up, are you, Jessie? You're not through being a human vacuum cleaner, or anything else, are you, girl?"

Laurie didn't agree with her parents that Jessie wasn't happy because she couldn't jump around as much or run as much or do anything as fast as she used to do.

"Wouldn't you be satisfied, Jessie, just lying in your sleeping basket, watching television with me, or sitting in our sun spot together? Who says everyone has to always run around fast, rushing everywhere?"

Laurie heard the dog's paws click across the tiled floors as Jessie sought a private place to enjoy her bone.

"I'm home, honey," her mother called from the front door, but Laurie didn't run to greet her. Instead, she fled up the back stairs to her room. The memories of this morning's conversation lingered with her. She didn't want to start it again.

"I'll be down in a little while," she called back to her mother after "Laurie, are you home?" traveled up the steps.

Instead, she sat down at her writing desk and took her slate and stylus from the drawer. She always felt better when she told Grandmom Beatrice what was on her mind. Her grandmother had learned braille years ago, before her poor health forced her into a nursing home in Florida. She and Grandpop had lived in Florida for years before he died. They had friends there, and two other daughters who visited often.

"But you're not even blind," Laurie had protested when her grandmother got her own slate and stylus.

"We'll always be able to write to each other this way, Sweetcake," her grandmother had answered. She had kept her promise by writing often. Grandmom Beatrice used braille as well as Laurie did, and all her raised dots that formed letters were punched in perfectly on the paper with her own pointed stylus and the slate that looked like a ruler with holes in it.

At the beginning, Grandmom told her that she had trouble learning the arrangement of dots that made up the letters of the alphabet and punching in the holes for the right letters, because for so many years she was used to writing so that she could read with her eyes. But once she got used to reading with her fingertips, she told Laurie, "it's just like learning another language in school."

Unlike Katherine, who left all her notes written up and down her bedroom walls, Laurie poured her thoughts onto the paper in front of her. She used the slate to hold down the paper and the stylus to punch in the holes that would form the raised dots that turned into words.

Dear Grandmom,

I hope you're feeling okay and you like your new roommate better. Maybe if you tell her to sleep on her side, she won't snore as loud. Someone said that on the radio. It's Jessie's birthday today and we're having the usual party, though Mom and Dad aren't as excited about it as they were last year.

Jessie is going to be 12 years old. Remember when she wandered into our house one day? Of course, I don't remember that, but Dad says you were there, and he always tells us Jessie's story on her birthday, how she walked up the front steps of our house and how her beagle ears were longer than her face and muddy, and how she had those big thoughtful brown eyes that Dad says beagles had as if she was thinking of something important. But her tail kept wagging. And then Dad called the animal shelter to see if a lost dog was reported and even watched the ads in the newspapers, but after a week, Jessie was

7

ours. I was only six months old, so Dad said it was like getting two babies at once.

So you'd think that Dad would be the last one to say what he said this morning and to do what he wants to do. Just because Jessie isn't young anymore and just because she has arthritis and just because she has bad days, sometimes, Dad keeps talking about putting Jessie to sleep. Forever. Even Mom agrees. She says we don't want to be cruel to Jessie. She says if Jessie is suffering too much, it would be kinder to take that suffering away. Jessie is going to be 84 years old in dog years today. Mom says she's had a beautiful life and that when animals can't use their legs properly, they lose a great part of their existence.

I can't stop thinking about that, Grandmom, about ending Jessie's life. I'm not sure how she feels about that either, and since I can't ask her and she can't tell me, I don't know how we can ever know. And now in another hour, I've got to go to Jessie's birthday party, only how can I blow out the candles for her like I usually do and cut her a big piece of cake, when it might be her last birthday party.

Thanks for the box of bubble gum.
Mom says she thinks it was enough to
last a whole year and by then, I shouldn't
have any teeth left if I chew it all.

Love you.

Laurie

Laurie left the writing table and walked over
to the closet. She sorted through her clothes,
touching the braille tags that told her what color
or print each of the clothes were. She wanted to
wear something special to Jessie's party. Her
mother had taught her to mark her clothes and to
care about what she looked like and what she
wore. Yellow was her favorite color. It made her
joyful and bright, just like the sun when it came
out. Laurie needed brightness today. She picked
out a yellow blouse and blue baggy pants.

"Blue looks so good on you," her best friend,
Betsy, always told her. "It matches your eyes."

It was perfectly satisfactory to Laurie that her
eyes were the color of her soft blue blanket that
covered her at night.

"How you doing, honey?" her mother's voice
asked from the doorway. "I'm sorry I got home
so late. I wanted to pick up Jessie's birthday cake
so Dad wouldn't have to do it. You know how tired
he's been lately."

Tired and grumpy, Laurie thought, after her
mother left. But she understood why he was so

worried. Every day he went to work, he didn't know if he was going to have a job. The computer company he worked for was on the verge of bankruptcy. But that didn't make it okay for her father to take out his bad mood on Jessie. If he didn't like getting up each morning to go to work, that didn't mean Jessie felt the same way.

"I bought Jessie her favorite meat bone," Betsy said, when she arrived for the party. She was fifteen minutes late. Betsy was always late, even to birthday parties. It was as if she didn't have a clock set right in her whole house. She unwrapped the gift. "My mom cooked the soup and it's not even her soup day, but she wanted Jessie to have a special taste."

It wasn't long before Laurie heard Jessie munching on the bone. They even had some fun with Katherine when she called to wish Jessie a happy birthday.

"Did you hear her?" Laurie asked, when she put the telephone receiver near Jessie's ear.

"It sounds like she's chipping away at cement." Katherine laughed. "How's she doing?"

"Okay," Laurie answered. She felt it wasn't exactly a lie. Right now, with her favorite bone in front of her, Jessie seemed her old self.

Even Grandmom Beatrice remembered. She insisted on singing "Happy Birthday" to Jessie from the telephone, just the way she sang it to everyone else in the family when it was their turn.

"Is she ready yet?" Laurie's mother finally called from the kitchen.

The gnawing stopped. It was as if Jessie knew the lit candles and the cake coming into the living room were for her. Laurie's father came home from work just as they were blowing out the candles.

"You made twelve years old, didn't you, old dog," he said, as he sat down at the table with them.

But he said it as if he hadn't expected that she would.

Laurie pushed away her plate with the half-eaten cake on it. Her appetite disappeared as she wondered if everybody around the table was thinking the same thing — that this might be the last birthday party for Jessie.

Only Jessie was unaware of anything but the piece of birthday cake she was slurping up from the plate. She didn't seem to mind that Laurie's father had forgotten her birthday story this year.

2

The next day in the school lunch line, Laurie realized someone was in front of her, blocking her way. She knew it even before her white traveling cane bumped into the immovable object. And she knew it was Josephine.

"Would you please get out of my way," Laurie asked as she moved into the lunch line. She slid the cane from side to side but didn't hit anything. Yet she knew Josephine was still there, waiting, taunting her. Laurie could hear the heavy breathing and the giggles. There were others laughing around her in the lunchroom.

"I'm coming through," Laurie warned as she balanced the tray, using the cane to clear a path.

"Are you sure you can't see? You're looking right at me," Josephine said. Her voice was loud and close. Laurie could feel Josephine's breath upon her face. She smelled from peppermint chewing gum. Laurie heard the clicking sound as the gum smacked around in Josephine's mouth.

"What do you expect me to do," Laurie shouted back. "Look somewhere else?"

"Oooh, what a temper," Josephine mimicked.

"Cut it out, will you, Josephine." It was Betsy's voice, coming from above and behind, and it was even louder than Josephine's. Betsy was taller than Laurie. In fact, when anyone met her, they thought she was in eighth grade, not sixth with Laurie.

"I'm not doing anything," Josephine answered. "I'm just standing here waiting for my lunch, minding my own business. What's wrong with that?"

"You're blocking her way on purpose, that's what. You're playing your stupid games again, Josephine, jumping in front of her cane."

Though Laurie appreciated Betsy's help, she felt uncomfortable listening to two people talk about her as if she weren't there. Betsy took her arm and pushed her forward, but Laurie pulled away. "I don't need any help," she told her, gently.

"You sure look like you need help to me," Josephine muttered, loud enough for everyone around them to hear. And then more quietly, "I'll be back later."

"She's just a jerk anyway," Betsy tried to comfort Laurie when they were finally seated at the lunch table. "How come you put so much ketchup on your french fries? I thought you didn't like ketchup."

It wasn't difficult for them to figure out who put the ketchup there.

"Just don't pay any attention to her, Laurie," Betsy repeated. "She doesn't get along with anybody."

"Maybe. But I seem to be the one she's always hanging around. What does she look like?" Laurie asked. She wanted to know about Josephine the way Josephine seemed to know about her. She needed to know about her eyes, if they were as mean-looking as her voice sounded. And her face — was it as ugly as the words that popped out from her mouth?

"She's got mousy, short brown hair," Betsy told her after she relieved Laurie's plate of the ketchuped french fries. "And dark eyes . . . I never see her smile. She always looks like she's ready for a fight. She walks just like a guy. You know, clumping down the hallway." Betsy gave Laurie one of her cupcakes. "She always wears these short white ankle socks. If I had legs like hers, I'd cover them up real fast."

Laurie was disappointed to find that knowing what Josephine looked like didn't make her feel any better.

"Baker Elementary had better food, don't you think?" Betsy asked.

"It sure did." The way Laurie felt right now, Baker had nicer people, nicer everything. She and Betsy had gone to Baker together since kindergarten. It was a smaller school than Bradley and it seemed everybody lived near everybody else. But then last year at the end of the marking period, Baker closed down. All the students merged with the larger Bradley School, and now they were bused to classes.

Everything had changed at Bradley. There were more students in the hallways crowding each other, and so much to learn about the long hallways and classrooms. Betsy and Laurie kept getting lost, and the first few days they were both late to wherever they were going. And then, of course, there was Josephine.

"My dad is taking Jessie to the veterinarian today," Laurie told Betsy as they entered biology class. It was the only class they had together, and they chose seats next to each other.

"He's not going to put her to sleep today, is he?" Betsy asked. The pain in Betsy's voice added to her own brought tears to Laurie's eyes.

"He promised that if the news isn't good and Dr. Nick says there's no hope, he'll wait and tell me. So I can say good-bye to Jessie. Though I don't know how I could ever do that, say good-bye to her that way. I wish I knew how Jessie felt about things like that."

She knew how Jessie felt about going outside or getting a bone or taking a walk, because she wagged her tail and started panting, but she had never discussed dying with Jessie. Jessie didn't even know the word. Later, as Laurie put her gloves on at the lab table, she wondered how her parents could be so certain that Jessie didn't like her life the way it was. It sure didn't look like she was suffering this morning. Even though she was walking slowly, Jessie managed to steal a piece of toast off the breakfast table. She washed it down with the bowl of milk Laurie's father had poured for his cereal and left sitting there. Jessie had managed to slurp it empty with her long tongue.

"Today, we're going to dissect a worm," Mr. Stevens announced.

"Yuk," Betsy whispered nearby. "This worm stinks."

It was the kind of whisper that traveled up to the front of the class.

"That's formaldehyde you smell," Mr. Stevens explained. "We store the worms in that chemical to preserve them."

Laurie felt comfortable in Mr. Stevens's class because he always explained everything carefully and repeated it just in case someone didn't understand. She took her dissecting kit and opened it, then lined up her scalpel scissors and dissecting needles and pins, along with the dissecting tray. Though she tried to listen to Mr. Stevens's instructions, her mind drifted away from the worm. She felt her braille wristwatch and wondered if Jessie was sitting on Dr. Nick's examining table, or if the examination was already finished.

"Are you doing okay, Betsy?" Mr. Stevens asked.

"I think I'm going to throw up," she answered honestly, before she had to go out into the hall to get a drink of water.

For Laurie, it was just like cutting the apples or pears she sliced at home when she made fruit salad. Her mother had taught her how to cut fruit and vegetables carefully without hurting herself, and her father, who was the better cook, had taught her about the oven and how to use it. In fact, she and Betsy had learned together. But Betsy managed to get sick every time they had to cut up something in biology class.

"I could hardly keep my mind on that dumb worm," Betsy said after class. "I kept thinking about Jessie. Do you want me to come home with you today? My mom made an appointment to get my hair cut, but I told her I don't want it short anyway."

Betsy's blond hair reached down to her waist, unlike Laurie's short dark hair, which felt as soft as nighttime.

"I'll be okay," Laurie tried to reassure Betsy. But as the hours dragged by she wasn't as certain.

She touched her watch often and wondered if her mother was watching the clock as well. She waitressed at a nearby restaurant and always complained that her feet bothered her at the end of her working shift.

The bus stop was two blocks from Laurie's home. After school, she walked them slowly. Usually she could hear Jessie's beagle bark shouting hello as she approached the houses a block away. Jessie always barked when she heard the school bus pull up, as did most of the dogs on the block.

"There's something about a school bus and the mailman that drives her crazy," Laurie's dad would say every time Jessie took a flying leap to the front door when she heard the mailman open the mailbox.

As Laurie approached the second block, she listened, but heard nothing. Each step that brought her closer to home increased her fear that Jessie wouldn't be there waiting for her. She almost felt like walking around the block one more time, just so she wouldn't have to know.

"She's gone," Laurie thought. "They've left her at Dr. Nick's. They're waiting for me to say goodbye."

She could barely turn the doorknob when she reached her front door. But when Laurie walked into the living room, she heard Jessie's deep snoring, and found her fast asleep in her basket. Jessie's snoring could wake up everyone in the house when she got into it, yet it was unusual, no matter how deep her sleep, that she didn't hear the front door open.

"Did Dr. Nick give you something to make you sleepy?" Laurie asked, so delighted to see her that she couldn't help rubbing the dog's ears, even though she knew it wasn't smart to disturb a sleeping dog.

Later, she found out the news wasn't all good.

"There's some new medication," her father told her as they washed the dishes together after dinner. "It'll take a couple of months to see if it will work. And if it does, she'll probably have to be on it the rest of her life."

Laurie didn't understand why her father's voice sounded so serious. Wasn't this the good news they had been hoping for?

"It's going to cost a lot of money," her father continued. He didn't sound as if he were enjoying the conversation either. "Truthfully, Laurie, I don't know how we're going to do it. And Dr. Nick can't guarantee anything. You know how hard your mother and I are working to keep Katherine in college, and then just about when we get finished, you'll be going. Every penny counts. I don't even know how long my job is going to last.

They laid off two hundred more people today."

"Isn't Jessie worth saving?" Laurie pleaded.

"It's going to take a big sacrifice from all of us," her mother added as she put away the dried dishes. "And what if it doesn't work? Honey, this isn't easy for any of us."

Laurie couldn't listen to any more of it. She ran from the room, up the steps into her bedroom, as if to run away from all truths she couldn't face.

Later, when she helped lift Jessie into her bed and snuggled close to her warm body, Laurie had to admit they were right about one thing. Jessie was an old dog. Laurie didn't feel as much fat on her bones as she had when Jessie was a puppy, and her breath had an odor to it. Dr. Nick said it was from some bad teeth that would fall out by themselves. The inside of Jessie's ears needed cleaning more often now. And then there was the arthritis.

"If you don't give up, then I won't give up on you either, Jessie," Laurie vowed as they sat resting against the pillows, sharing some pistachio nuts that Laurie kept in a jar next to the bed. "I'll take care of the rest," she promised.

After Jessie spit out the shells and Laurie threw them in the garbage can, they settled down under the blankets.

"I promise you, Jessie, you're going to have all the medicine you need to get better."

Laurie believed in keeping promises, but even as she made this one, and even as she heard Jessie's contented breathing next to her, she knew she had made a promise that would be difficult to keep.

3

"Where's Mr. Stevens?" Betsy asked when they walked into biology class at the end of the week.

"He broke his leg," Johnny Hayes answered. His voice sounded as if it were sliding up and down a musical scale. Sometimes it got deep without warning, and sometimes it sounded like a girl's. "Mr. Williams is a permanent substitute."

"Johnny's voice is changing," Betsy whispered as they sat down at their desks. "My brother's voice is doing the same thing."

"What does Mr. Williams look like?" Laurie whispered. She liked to know as much as she could about her teachers and the people in her class. Betsy had already told her that Johnny Hayes had dark hair like her own, green eyes lighter than the grass, and a bunch of freckles on his nose. Betsy also reported that he always looked as if he was thinking of something important when he looked Laurie's way.

"He's tall," Betsy said. "And real thin. And he's got a mustache. He keeps smoothing it down with one hand while he's going through some papers on his desk. His hair is sort of reddish brown."

Betsy always gave good descriptions. She noticed details about people that most people didn't even see. She also knew that once she described something to her, Laurie never forgot it. It stuck right in her memory where Betsy had placed it. Laurie felt lucky to have such a good friend.

"My name is Mr. Williams," the substitute teacher introduced himself before they began their lab work. "I'll be taking Mr. Stevens's place until he has recuperated."

Laurie found it difficult to concentrate as she opened her notebook and took out her slate and stylus to take her notes. Her after-school plans kept getting in her way. Today was the day she had promised herself she would begin to look for a job, something to do that would bring in the extra money needed for Jessie's medicine.

"You're Laurie, aren't you?" Mr. Williams asked as she got up to walk over to the lab tables with the others.

Laurie nodded. Betsy was right. He was tall. His words traveled from way above her head. The distance became shorter as Mr. Williams bent down. "I've got something special for you to do," he told her. "I'd like you to write a report for homework about everything you've read about the worm, and then we can discuss it later."

Laurie left her desk and walked over to the reading section that Mr. Stevens had set up in the room. There were all kinds of books, with a section in braille. "Here it is," Mr. Williams said as he put the book in her hands. She wanted to tell him she could have found it herself, but decided it was his first day and he probably had more important things on his mind.

Laurie's fingers traveled swiftly over the pages while Betsy and the others took their places behind the lab tables and began to work on the worms. She never had enjoyed the worms before, but today she truly wished she were with everybody else, and she didn't understand why she wasn't. She thought perhaps Mr. Williams was giving her a special assignment.

"What did he do that for?" Betsy asked when the bell rang for dismissal.

"Beats me," Laurie answered.

"Glenda told me that this is Mr. Williams's first job as a teacher, and he dropped all the papers in her class. He even forgot to take attendance." But before Betsy could finish the gossip she had collected, Mr. Williams's voice interrupted their conversation in the hallway.

"I'll walk you to the bus, Laurie," he said. And then Laurie understood everything. She understood it as he walked close by her side down the hallway and opened the doors for her and kept saying, "Watch it, Laurie. There's a door here. A step here," though her long white cane told her everything she needed to know. All she had to do was move it back and forth in front of her to see if there were any steps, or trash cans or anything else in her way. She didn't know Mr. Williams well enough to tell him any of that, and maybe he wouldn't even believe her if she did.

They waited apart from the other students for the bus to arrive. Mr. Williams was taking care of her as if she were a little child who couldn't find her own way. He didn't think she could make it to the bus safely. He didn't even think she could get on it alone. And he sure didn't believe she could cut up a worm without cutting herself. In that moment of understanding, for the first time since she was born, Laurie felt her blindness. Mr. Williams had done that to her.

"I hate being blind," she yelled as soon as she got into the empty house and slammed the door behind her. And she hated Mr. Williams for reminding her that she was.

Jessie's thumping tail reminded Laurie that she had more important things to do this afternoon than stand there feeling sorry for herself. She picked up a bottle she kept next to the Milk-Bone jar and opened it. Quickly she popped one of the magic pills into Jessie's mouth.

"We both deserve a treat after today," she smiled as she handed Jessie her bone and took an

25

ice cream pop from the freezer for herself. Then she wrote a note to her mother. There was always a slate and stylus on the kitchen table and a few around the house because everybody left notes for each other.

"Betsy and I are going bicycle riding," she wrote, "to that new bicycle shop off Main Street. Betsy's bicycle was stolen last week and her parents said she could pick out another one. So she's going to start looking." Betsy had trouble making up her mind when she had to choose, even when they went to a movie. It would take a long time before she could even decide which candy bar to buy at the refreshment stand.

What Laurie didn't tell her mother was that she intended to see if she could get a job at the bicycle shop, or anywhere else they passed by that seemed interesting. Every time she had brought up the possibility during the past week, her mother had disappointed her by saying, "You're too young, Laurie. No one will hire you." Her mother usually encouraged her to try new things. Only Betsy knew of her plans.

Laurie moved her bicycle from the garage to the driveway. She put her white cane in a basket attached to the back. The bicycle had two seats on it, and two sets of pedals. Her father had taught her to ride a bicycle when she was seven years old, and after school that was her favorite pastime. Betsy usually rode with her, or sometimes one of her parents would come along. There had been a single bicycle for her when she was very young, almost too young to remember. Her father had tied a rope between his bicycle and her own to teach her, but she had fallen, and never wanted to ride by herself again.

"Why did Mr. Williams walk you to the bus?" Betsy asked from the front seat as they rode down the street. "Didn't you feel good?"

"Nothing was wrong with me," Laurie answered. "I think something's wrong with Mr. Williams. He didn't think I could find the bus."

"Are you kidding? Why would he think something stupid like that?"

"Because I'm blind, silly," Laurie answered, at first annoyed that her friend had to be reminded.

She heard the giggle from the front seat as if they had just shared a special joke, and as usual it was contagious. Laurie joined Betsy's laughter as the warm fall sun fell on her body and the day's brightness renewed her energy. With two of them pumping on the pedals, they sped easily up the eight blocks to Main Street.

"Is it a big store?" Laurie asked after they locked their bicycle to a bar in front of it.

Laurie used her white cane to find the front door when Betsy opened it. She liked discovering new places to visit and learning about them. Betsy seemed to enjoy telling her about the new places as much as she enjoyed listening.

"Real big," Betsy answered. "It's as big as your backyard and mine put together. And there's a Help Wanted sign in the window. They've got hundreds of bicycles here stacked in lines everywhere and they're all different colors."

Laurie knew that meant they were going to be there for a long time, but she didn't mind. Betsy was patient with her curiosity, and now it was her turn to be patient with her friend.

"You go look and I'll stay here," she told Betsy, hoping that while she waited, she'd find the nerve to ask about the job opening. While she lingered, she felt the cool chrome of handlebars next to her. She rang the bell attached to it. There was no rust or rough edges on this bicycle. She could almost smell its newness.

"Can I help you?" a man asked.

"No, thank you," Laurie answered. "I was just waiting for my friend. She's looking for a bicycle."

"Which one is she?" the man asked. "Maybe I can help her."

"She's got blond hair in a braid," Laurie told him.

"Do you know which corner of the store she's in?"

The continuing questions made Laurie feel awkward, since she couldn't answer most of them. She had no idea where Betsy was, and she didn't know why this man would think she did. The white cane was standing right in front of him.

His presence began to make her feel uncomfortable so she moved away, but when she did, she bumped into the stack of bicycles standing in front of her. They crashed down upon each other, their noise echoing throughout the store.

"Oh, oh." Laurie winced. "I'm really sorry."

"Don't worry about it," the man answered. "People do it all the time. I'm going to move that display rack tomorrow. I'm just short of help right now. There, you see, they're all back where they were."

That's when Laurie realized she was talking to the owner of the store. She realized something else. He needed help. And she needed work.

"I'm looking for a job," she said. The words rushed out as if they were afraid they might not get the chance if they waited.

"What can you do?" the man asked. "You sound quite young."

Laurie was so nervous she barely heard his question. "I guess I can do whatever you want me to," she answered, though she doubted it very much. She had no working experience, but she could type, and her teachers always told her that she did that very well. The thought of Jessie's expensive medicine doubled her courage to continue. "My teachers say I learn very fast, and I got all A's last semester."

"All A's, huh?" The man sounded as if he was impressed.

She wanted to impress him more. "I've been riding a bicycle since I was seven years old," she told him, though she didn't tell him it was a bicycle built for two. "And I live nearby." She remembered her mother's words whenever Laurie decided to try something new: *When you decide you want something, you sure go after it.*

Laurie was going after it now with everything in her.

"How old are you?" the man asked.

Laurie was surprised that he couldn't tell. Most people said she looked exactly her age. Once, at a fair, she had gone to the man who sat on a stool guessing people's ages. He had told her it was easy to guess her age because she didn't look older and she didn't look younger. She looked exactly what she was.

"I'm twelve years old," she answered honestly, while she wished she could have been sixteen. Everybody that she knew who was sixteen seemed to be able to do so many things.

"How about coming back with your parents tomorrow and we can talk more about it. There are plenty of odd jobs around here, though not too many people want to take the time to learn about them. I like my work done just the way I want it to be done."

Laurie could tell by the man's voice that he would not be easy to work for.

"My name's George Salvadore," he said. "Everybody calls me George, though."

"Mine's Laurie Moss."

When Betsy and she left the store, they both began talking at once.

"There was an apple-red bicycle, but I think I like the green one, but that one might cost too much. Do you think I should get the red one?"

"He said I should bring back my parents. He actually told me to come back. Maybe I could work there. Do you think he was serious about hiring me for a real job?"

"What job?" Betsy asked.

"Apple red?" Laurie asked back.

But when they settled down in front of Laurie's house, Betsy asked seriously, "I need your help deciding, Laurie. Because they had the neatest green bicycle there, too. Right next to the red one. What do you think?"

"Green is a nice color," Laurie agreed. The grass was green and cool beneath her feet when she walked on it barefoot in the summer. She had once been afraid of the sometimes rough, sometimes surprisingly soft growth that wasn't there in the cold and then popped up suddenly when it got warm. Now she liked to run in it. Green was a cool color.

"The owner was real nice," Betsy continued. "He took so much time when I asked him questions and he knew everything about bicycles. He fixed somebody's broken chain right in front of me and it just took two minutes."

"What's so strange about that?" Laurie asked. "He owns a bicycle shop. He should know what to do about bicycles."

"I guess so," Betsy replied, though she didn't sound as certain. "I just never saw a blind person fix a bicycle, did you?"

Laurie's mouth dropped open in surprise. If George wasn't sighted, then he didn't know she was blind also. Laurie wondered how he would feel when he found out.

4

Laurie could feel the late October chill even through the closed windows of her bedroom. She was glad that Betsy was late today. The extra few minutes before they left for the movie gave her the chance to read Grandmom's letter, which had just come in the mail. She never failed to get excited when she found the envelope on her writing desk waiting for her. There was something wonderful about receiving a letter, an unexpected message that she could read over and over again, traveling hundreds of miles and arriving right at the doorstep.

Dear Laurie,
    I don't think I've slept five minutes since you told me about Jessie. Believe me, if I were up there, I'd tell your parents a thing or two about getting old. I'd tell them that just because things don't work as well, that doesn't mean they

don't work at all. So what if I'm a little crooked and wrinkled. I'll tell you a little secret, Laurie. I have this special magic mirror on my bureau and when I look into it, I don't see one wrinkle. I look as young as I ever did, but I wouldn't tell that to just anybody, because they wouldn't believe me.

And I'll tell you something else. There was this sunset last night. I sat there staring out my window for thirty solid minutes studying that miracle of life. Those colors. You know how we'd watch them together and I'd tell you about the purples and the blues and the leftover oranges all getting together for a splendid party to end the day.

(Laurie had her own ideas of what the colors of the sunset were like . . . yellow hot like the sun, orange like the pumpkin she cut faces into at Halloween, cool turquoise like some jewels on a belt, and blue like her soft blanket, warm and comfortable, a peaceful color.)

I sat there and enjoyed that moment as if I'd never seen it before. It's wonders like that, Laurie, that don't get old. In fact, right after I finish this letter, I'm going to write one to your parents to remind them of a few things.

I'm sending you in a separate package a box of bubble gum, two packages of licorice sticks, and two dozen Florida oranges. The oranges should make your mother feel good, since they're full of vitamin C and they're good for your teeth.

Don't worry about Jessie. We'll come up with something.

Love and Kisses,
Grandmom Beatrice

Laurie touched her braille watch impatiently as she waited for Betsy, who was unusually late. What Laurie hadn't gotten the chance to tell Grandmom, because she had been so busy, was that she had come up with something already. She was working at George's bicycle shop. George could hire her for only a couple of hours on Saturday and an hour Friday after school. Laurie had to make arrangements to get her working papers through her guidance counselor because she was underage and couldn't work without them.

"I can use another pair of hands," George had told her parents when they came with her for a real interview. This time everyone sat down in George's office. George's voice got serious when he told her parents, "I didn't really intend to hire Laurie, because she was too young. I just thought she wouldn't come back." And then he had said something really surprising. "But now that I know she's blind, it's even more important that I hire her. I think it's real important that blind adults show blind young people what they can do in the job market."

"I'm sorry I'm late," Betsy apologized as she rushed into the room. She sounded as if she were running. Betsy always said she was sorry, but Laurie didn't mind waiting the extra five or ten minutes. Because when Betsy finally got there, she always had an exciting story to tell about why she was late, and she didn't disappoint Laurie today.

"I would have been here earlier," she began, still out of breath, "but first I had this fight with my mom. You know how she's always asking me if the desks are comfortable. All the time, she wants to know, and she says the school should have left-handed desks for left-handed people. Baker did and now she wants the same thing at Bradley. I mean it's a new school for me, Laurie, and I told her I didn't want her to make a fuss over it."

By this time they were rushing out the front door toward the movie. Laurie grabbed her white cane that was hanging by the front door.

"Well, now she wants to go into school and complain because all the desks are right-handed. Can you imagine her doing that?"

"I sure wouldn't like my mom to do that," Laurie agreed. That was one of the reasons she wasn't saying anything about Mr. Williams and their daily walks to the bus. "At least there are other left-handed kids in the school," she tried to comfort Betsy. Laurie was the only blind student at Bradley, which gave Mr. Williams plenty of time to concentrate on her.

"You know how my mom is when she gets excited. Her face gets all red and her voice loud. They'll hear her in every classroom in the school."

Just as they approached the movie theater, Betsy offered some more news.

"I talked to Ellen on the telephone today. She told me Johnny Hayes is supposed to be seeing the same movie today that we are. Ellen is going to meet us there."

"I don't care if Johnny Hayes is here," Laurie protested, as they bought their ticket. Lately, Betsy was always telling her when Johnny Hayes was around, as if it mattered to her, as if she cared a hoot if he was or he wasn't. Anyway, Laurie didn't need anyone to tell her, because she could tell by the noise that traveled with him. Betsy told her once it was a set of keys attached to his belt.

"He has a key to get into the front door of his house and the back door and the garage and his next-door neighbor's house and for the lock on his bicycle and one for his roller skates, and he even has a set of keys that doesn't belong to anyone he knows. He found them on the sidewalk. He just likes to carry keys."

They had just settled into the soft cushiony chairs and begun to share the popcorn when the movie began, and the noise around them started almost at the same time.

"I'm over here," Ellen shouted from a row in front of them.

"So who cares?" someone answered back.

"We'll see you later," Betsy yelled over someone who was making noise sipping the last bit of soda from the can through a straw. But gradually, as the music played in front of them, things quieted down except for the sound of popcorn being munched.

"What's going on?" Laurie whispered to Betsy. "It's so quiet on the screen."

Sometimes Betsy forgot that she needed information, so Laurie had to ask.

"A man is walking into a bank. He's mean-looking," Betsy answered. "He's got a scar down his cheek and he's big. He's got muscles all over the place."

"What's the girl look like? She sounds so pretty. I bet she's tiny," Laurie whispered.

"She is real small. But she's got muscles, too. She's got on one of those gym leotards and she's bulging all over the place. The guy's carrying something in a box. I think he wants to blow up the place."

From that point on, except for some long periods of silence, Laurie kept track of the action by the conversation going on and the background music usually told her when something exciting or dangerous was going to happen. Every time it did there was plenty of noise coming from the screen, like gunshots and explosions and police sirens and people screaming.

In between the popcorn throwing and someone spilling soda that ran underneath Betsy's seat and Ellen calling back now and then, Laurie heard the keys jangling nearby, but she refused to ask Betsy where Johnny Hayes was sitting.

"He likes you," Betsy told her on the way home.

"Who?" Laurie pretended not to know, though they had the same conversation almost every day.

"You know who. Johnny Hayes was sitting in the row right behind us. He came in just when the picture started."

"So what?" Laurie could feel the flush race across her face.

"So he could have sat anywhere. But he didn't. He sat right near you. That's what. He always sits near you."

"He doesn't even talk to me. He's never said a word."

"Doesn't matter," Betsy insisted. "He's just shy."

Laurie knew more about Johnny than she was even letting Betsy know. She knew his father had died when he was young and his mother worked two jobs to support them, and he had all those keys because he was usually home alone. She knew all that because Ellen had told her. Once she found it out, she didn't feel it was something she should talk about. Just the way she wouldn't want someone to talk about her blindness when she wasn't there.

"Can you come over to my house?" Betsy asked, when they reached Laurie's home.

"I can't today. I've got to be at work at four o'clock. George has a shipment of bicycles coming in and he wants me to tag them. He's real fussy about my being on time."

"I sure wouldn't like that," Betsy said before she left.

Actually, Laurie didn't like it either. There were a lot of things she didn't like about George. He talked more than anybody else she knew and he always had something to say to her. George told her there were responsibilities about working at a job that nobody should forget. Like being on time. And liking what you do. And not being afraid to learn. And working hard because hard work was good for a person. Being independent and being able to take care of yourself were necessary. George used the word "necessary" just about every time she was around him.

George was already busy tagging the bicycles when Laurie got there. As soon as she entered the store, she bumped into a bicycle that wasn't there yesterday.

"Blind people aren't the only ones who bump into things when they're not paying attention," George scolded her as he helped her pick up the bicycle.

"I didn't see it there," she replied, though she guessed, by George's tone of voice, that he expected her to know where things were and to be careful.

His voice softened. "You just fill out the braille tags as I give you the information and then we'll tie them on the bicycle handles. That way I'll be able to tell the customers everything they need to know about the bicycles. Now just write carefully so I understand . . . I hate sloppiness."

"Okay, George," Laurie said as she wrote down what he told her. She guessed she must have said, "Okay, George," about twelve times that afternoon. She said okay when he told her that she should begin memorizing some of the tools on the shelves, as he told her what they were and where they were.

"I've memorized hundreds of them," he boasted. "I know what each tool does."

She said, "Okay, George," again when he showed her how he recorded his repair information on a cassette tape and tied it with an elastic band to the bicycle seat. "As I make repairs, I talk into the cassette, adding up the parts I sup-

41

plied and the length of time it took me to do the work. So when the customer comes back, I play the tape. And then I add up everything on my talking calculator. You could help me by making some of these tapes. I keep an extra set of records in braille."

"Why don't you just keep all of your repair records in braille?" Laurie asked. It seemed much easier to do it that way.

"Because that's the way I do things," George answered, firmly.

"Okay, George."

Working at George's and for George wasn't as easy as Laurie thought it would be as the days passed. Even though it was just an hour and a half here and a few hours there, she had to do plenty of listening and just as much thinking. And George always had a lecture about everything. She did a lot of her chores right, but George always made her feel it never was enough.

"You can do things because you've been taught to do them just the way everyone else is taught," he'd say whenever she made a mistake. One thing George didn't do: He didn't make any excuses for being blind.

Right on his desk he had a sign, with one line for the sighted, he told her, and one for those who read braille. "BEING BLIND IS RESPECTABLE," it read.

Even though she was tired when she finished

on weekends, and feeling that she couldn't stand to hear one more word come out of George's mouth, it was worth all the work when she opened the front door of her house and heard Jessie's barking. Laurie placed all the money she earned in the bank to add to the monthly checks paid to Dr. Nick.

"Can you take her out for a walk?" her mother asked at the end of Laurie's fourth week on the job. "I actually think Jessie wants to go walking today."

That was great news. Laurie grabbed the leash and her white cane. She heard Jessie's paws crunch the leaves as she tugged on the leash, as if she wanted to go faster. Fall was Jessie's favorite time of year anyway. Her long ears dragged the leaves with her as she sniffed along the ground. And when they got home Laurie had to carefully pull the leaves off Jessie's body.

But even as she did, she wondered how long both of them could keep doing what they were doing. She wondered if Jessie found it as difficult to get up in the morning as she found it to spend another day working for George.

5

Laurie had spent the whole month of November learning how to put on the roller skates that Grandmom Beatrice had sent her. She had been careful to learn how to tighten the skates with her key, but her usual enthusiasm for trying something new was missing. She was still afraid to use them.

Everybody skated after school at this time of year. Some of her classmates even skated to school. But Laurie had never wanted to skate, never asked for them. Standing there with wobbly legs in front of her house, she wished Grandmom Beatrice had decided to send her another present instead of this one. But knowing Grandmom, there was a reason for everything she did.

"Just don't go in the street," her mother warned right before she went outside. "And be careful."

Her mother always said "Be careful," just the way Betsy's mother did, though Betsy's mother sometimes was worse. She'd stand there for ten

44

minutes giving both of them all kinds of things to be afraid of that they had never thought of before.

The doubts lingered as Laurie started down the sidewalk. Her cane led the way as she slowly steadied her legs. The day was crisp, and most of the leaves were gone as she pushed her skates over the cement sidewalk. She didn't feel as comfortable as she would on her two-seated bicycle or if Betsy had been able to come with her. But Betsy was in bed with a sore throat, and Grandmom's letter let Laurie know that she expected the skates to be used right away.

"I'll call you at the end of the week and see how you like them," Grandmom Beatrice had written.

Laurie could never lie to Grandmom, and neither could anyone else in the family. Even though Grandmom was miles away and even though her voice wasn't as strong as it used to be, she could still make everybody in the house scurry about when she gave an order. "I have spoken," she'd say. And that was that.

The sidewalk wasn't smooth and each time Laurie hit a bump, her arms reached out to steady herself. There were more bumps in the sidewalk than she ever remembered when walking. Too many bumps. Too many stops and starts. She didn't feel certain about herself or what she was doing.

In fact, if she admitted it, she didn't feel certain anymore about anything the way she used to. Certainly, Mr. Williams didn't believe in what she could do. "You'd better not do this," he'd say about one thing, or "Should you do this?" he'd ask about another, until Laurie wondered if he felt she could do anything by herself. To make matters worse, none of the teachers at Bradley seemed to feel comfortable with her. She wondered if they had ever had a blind student in their classes before.

She heard a set of keys jangle as she hit the bump in front of her that sent her spilling forward on her knees.

"Are you okay?" Johnny Hayes's voice only made Laurie feel worse.

"Sure, I'm okay. Why shouldn't I be okay?" Laurie answered. Two throbbing knees and a missing cane that had flown out of her hands made things far from okay as Laurie sat there on the ground.

The keys jangled again. "Here's your cane, Laurie," Johnny Hayes offered, as he handed it to her. "Do you need help getting up?"

The word "help" sent renewed energy into Laurie's legs. Mr. Williams was giving her too much help and he was getting others around her to help, and today, this very minute, that was the last thing she wanted.

"I can get up myself," she said. "So you can go now." But the roller skates refused to obey. They kept sliding back and forth, making it impossible for Laurie to regain her balance.

She waited to hear the sound of the keys travel in another direction, but there was no sign of that. Johnny was standing there watching her. She moved her white cane and it bumped into his shoe.

Then she felt his hand take her own and pull her upright. "I knocked my front tooth out when I was a kid," he said. "I was on my roller skates and it wasn't even my first time. Everybody falls."

Then the keys jangled in the opposite direction. Laurie sat down on a nearby stoop and took off the roller skates. She didn't care if Johnny Hayes fell or if everybody else in her classroom did. She didn't like the feeling of losing control like that. When she got home she threw the roller skates in the closet, in the back, where all the other things she didn't use were kept.

Betsy was interested in the two Band-Aids on her knees the next day in the lunchroom.

"Boy, that must hurt," she said. "You should have waited until I could have gone with you."

It was the wrong thing to say today, especially after Mr. Williams had suggested Laurie sit in the reading section again while they did some more dissecting.

"I don't need someone to go with me everywhere I go," Laurie snapped back.

"How come you have that glob of mustard on your potatoes?" Betsy asked. And then before Laurie could answer, she muttered, "That Josephine. I've got to tell her a thing or two."

"Don't tell her anything for me. I'll take care of it myself." The good mood Laurie had awakened with was shattered. She didn't really have any idea how she would take care of Josephine, who was bigger and tougher and nastier than anyone she had ever met before.

"What are you fighting with me for?" Betsy asked. "I didn't put the mustard on your potatoes."

"I'm sorry," Laurie apologized. "I just wish I didn't have to come to Bradley one more day."

"Well, next week should be fun anyway. I can't wait to go on the planetarium trip," Betsy said, as they shared some popcorn. "At least we won't be in school that day."

"What planetarium trip?" Laurie asked.

"Mr. Williams wrote it on the board this morning. Didn't he tell you about the permission slip you'll need?"

"He must have forgotten," Laurie replied. Mr. Williams did that a lot. He forgot that when he wrote things on the blackboard, Laurie didn't know they were there unless he or someone else told her about them. She couldn't read his mind.

Once out of school at the end of the day, Laurie's life changed. She did what she had to do without anybody helping her. She ran errands for her mother, listened to music on the radio or her tapes, worked at George's, and did her homework.

She did all of her homework on her braille-writer. It looked just like a regular typewriter, except that it had six keys on it and it typed everything out in braille. Mr. Stevens had been a special education teacher and he knew braille. Mr. Williams was supposed to hand her homework to Ms. Allen, the transcriptionist, who changed all Laurie's schoolwork from braille to print. But Laurie didn't have to ask anybody to do anything for her at home, and nobody in the family asked her if she needed help. Except on special occasions when everybody got busy helping everybody else. Like the sleepover that Laurie was having for Betsy and Ellen tonight.

Laurie and her mother went to the food market to shop.

"I'll make some meatballs for tonight," her mother said. "Betsy loves my spaghetti sauce."

Her mother hurried down the aisles, with Laurie close behind.

"I think Jessie is getting better," Laurie said hopefully. "Did you hear Dad this morning? He was yelling because he couldn't find his socks." Laurie picked out a head of lettuce and some grapes. The fruit felt cool beneath her hands as she put it in the cart. By their shapes she could easily tell what was in front of her, just as she could easily handle the dissecting kit. Except the longer Mr. Williams kept her away from everything, the less confidence she had that she could do it when she had to. All she hoped for was Mr. Stevens's quick recovery.

"Jessie does seem to be getting around," her mother agreed. "But truthfully, honey, Dad and I are concerned about you. Is something wrong at Bradley? You just don't seem as happy there as you did at Baker Elementary."

Visions of her mother marching to school the way Betsy's did just about every day, fighting for the left-handed desks, stopped the truth behind her lips.

"I like the school, Mom," she told her. "I really love it. Everything's great."

"Well, maybe it's the work. Dad and I wonder if is isn't too much, your working at the bicycle shop. We don't want your grades to suffer."

"I love that, too, Mom, honest," Laurie lied. Actually, she dreaded going in now. Even though the money was appreciated at the end of the week, putting up with George's lectures and George's nagging and George's instructions was making every hour's work seem like a day.

As for the suffering grades, Laurie had an idea that they had already suffered. Mr. Williams always forgot to have Ms. Allen prepare her tests ahead of time in braille, like Laurie's other teachers did. Instead, he gave her the tests in study class, in the back of the room, but no matter how quietly she tried to answer, she knew her classmates sitting nearby heard her voice and his questions. She never could concentrate doing it like that.

"Do you need some spaghetti?" she asked her mother, shaking the box. Laurie knew the aisles, and each shelf and what was on it. They had gone shopping in the same supermarket since she was a little girl.

They had just time enough to put on the pot of meat sauce and get the spaghetti boiling before Ellen arrived for the sleepover. Betsy came a half-hour late. "I didn't know what time it was," she explained.

A sleepover was a big responsibility. It was as if Jessie felt so, too, because she was everywhere Laurie went. At the kitchen table when they ate dinner, she begged. Nobody felt like scolding her, because they were so glad to see her up to her old tricks.

After dinner and dessert and some television and listening to tapes and painting fingernails, they were ready for games.

"The finger game first," Betsy pleaded. "I haven't played that for a long time."

"I don't know how to play it," Ellen admitted.

"It's easy," Laurie said. "There are six things in this basket with the cover over it. My mom put them there. You just reach in the basket, keep your eyes shut, and guess what you're feeling when you take out whatever's in there."

"It's a lemon," Ellen giggled on her first try.

"Sorry. It's an egg," Betsy laughed. "Let me try now. I've got a piece of string."

"No, you don't," Laurie told her when she felt it. "It's a piece of ribbon."

"You're right," Betsy said, when she opened her eyes.

Laurie knew the apple wasn't an orange because it had a stem.

Ellen did better with the foot game. "I never played games like this before," she said as she felt toothpicks and sandpaper on the cookie tin beneath her toes and tried to identify them.

Betsy was the best on smells. The different jars, prepared beforehand by Laurie's mother, had different smelly objects in them, like cheese and soap and banana peels and an open bottle of nail polish. Betsy sailed through guessing them. But Laurie didn't like any of the games as much as Monopoly. Her set had braille markings, and she would have played all night if her mother hadn't come in to turn off the light.

In the dark, they wrote down the sounds they heard in the night to see who could get the longest list. Ellen's included a ringing telephone and a car rushing down the block. Betsy heard a creaking step and the squeaking bed beneath her. Laurie listed their breathing, the rustle of their pajamas, the ticking clock.

It had become the best sleepover she ever had,

until Betsy came back from the bathroom.

"I think something's wrong with Jessie," Betsy said. "She's limping when she walks."

Laurie's heart felt as if it relocated swiftly to her stomach.

"Are you sure?" she asked. "Maybe she's just stiff. Sometimes when she's all curled up sleeping, it takes her a while to get going."

"Nope. I'm sure. She's limping."

When Laurie checked downstairs, she found Betsy was right. Jessie appeared restless, unable to stay in her basket for long. Each time she came out of it, Laurie heard the uneven sound of her paws as she limped toward her.

"Tomorrow we'll go to Dr. Nick's," Laurie soothed her friend. "He'll make you feel better, Jessie. He always does, doesn't he?" She kissed the long ears and the thumping tail wagged as if Jessie understood.

After Ellen and Betsy fell asleep, Laurie returned to her writing desk in the dark. She took out her slate and stylus and poured out her doubts to her grandmother.

Dear Grandmom Beatrice:

I was just missing you and wanted you to know that I don't care if you're wrinkled and crooked and slow or anything else that you said in your last letter. I know what you mean about watching sunsets and it's like seeing it for the first time, because I feel that way about rainstorms. They sound so great hitting the windowpanes and feel so cool on my skin. I love to walk in them.

I guess some people just don't understand things like that, Grandmom, like you and me, so that's why I'm real lucky because I know you're there understanding everything I feel. And I guess I wanted you to know I'm here feeling the same things.

Like about Jessie. Sometimes on her good days I think everything is going to be okay, but then on her bad days, I'm not sure of anything at all. I mean, how do you know when it's time to say goodbye to someone you love?

You can start keeping score again in our new tournament. This time I get the Xs.

Love, Laurie

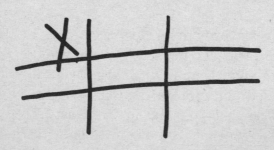

Later, she tried to sleep, but thoughts of another visit to Dr. Nick and another bill and more worried discussions between her parents kept her eyelids from closing restfully.

Since she was awake anyway, she decided it would be all right to think about Johnny Hayes and how nice he was on the day of the big roller-skating fall. She didn't even mind that he jangled when he walked.

6

Laurie couldn't believe it. She had flunked the big biology test with a low 60. Betsy had gotten an 85. Almost everyone that she talked to had passed.

The week of the test had been a busy one. There had been an extra trip to Dr. Nick's after the sleepover, to take out a sticker from Jessie's paw. Then George had decided to restack his supply shelves. And to top it all off, she and Josephine had another skirmish when Josephine shut the door to the girls' room in Laurie's face so that she bumped into it.

In spite of everything going on, Laurie felt she had managed to study enough. At least, the book had been in front of her for hours, her fingers resting on the pages, though they didn't move across it often. She couldn't concentrate. The facts in the book weren't sticking in her mind. What was remaining there was Mr. Williams, and how he would give her the test. As usual, everyone else would write out their answers. As usual, he would ask her the questions in the study class or wherever else he could fit it into his busy life. She never knew when or where. But she knew by this time that it would be with others listening around them.

Today, she couldn't stop herself from thinking of that number, 60, and how it would pull her average down. She thought of it through Mr. Williams's explanation of the planctarium they were about to visit and she thought of it through the bus ride there.

"You sure are quiet today," Betsy said. "I didn't tell you Johnny Hayes is sitting across from us staring at you. I think he wants to say something."

"How do you know he wants to say anything? If he did, he would," Laurie assured her.

"I can tell. You can always tell when somebody wants to say something. They just get that look in their eyes."

Laurie was getting tired of these forecasts about Johnny Hayes and what Betsy thought he was about to do. One day she said he looked like he was going to come over to them at the mall. Another time she said he got right up to Laurie's side but then turned around real fast and walked away.

"Why don't you say something to him?" Betsy said as they got off the bus.

"What am I going to say?" Laurie asked.

"Ask him who won the baseball game yesterday. I saw him playing after school near the parking lot."

"But I don't care who won the game," Laurie answered, honestly. That was the best thing about having a friend like Betsy. They could be honest with each other.

"That doesn't have anything to do with it. You pretend you care."

"Why should I pretend I care?"

"So you'll have something to talk about."

"But why do I have to talk about something I don't want to talk about?"

"Because he'll want to talk about it. Boys always want to talk about baseball."

"I don't like pretending. Why wouldn't he talk about something I wanted to talk about?"

"Gosh, Laurie, you sure are in a rotten mood today," Betsy shot back.

Maybe she was. But she still didn't see why she had to talk about baseball. Still, she didn't have a chance to do anything about it even if she wanted to. Mr. Williams was by her side again, as if he were glued to her.

"Be careful. There's a step over there. You're coming to a curb. Don't trip and don't walk too fast."

"Sure, Mr. Williams. I'm fine, Mr. Williams." She knew that even though her mother had signed the consent form for her to go on the class trip,

Mr. Williams wasn't comfortable having her there. Laurie almost felt sorry for him. From the time they had gotten on the bus until now, when they got off, he had kept checking on her to see if she was all right. She didn't know what he was worried about or what he thought could happen to her that couldn't happen to anyone else on the bus. She knew where the emergency door was, and she knew how to use it.

"I see the curb," she tried to reassure him as she tapped it with her cane. But she knew he didn't believe her anyway.

Once inside and seated in the auditorium next to Betsy, Laurie heard Mr. Williams give instructions to everyone.

"Put on the earphones," he said. "You'll be told about everything you're seeing on the screen above your heads."

Laurie put on her earphones, but just as the voice inside them spoke in a soft, clear voice, she felt someone tap her on the shoulder. It was Mr. Williams, sitting next to her.

"You won't need the earphones, Laurie," he said. "I'll tell you something about what the others are seeing. I want you to get the most out of this trip."

"They're telling me in here." Laurie pointed to the earphones.

"I know they are. But I think that might only confuse you. I could give you more information."

He whispered, "You remember, I told you a planet is a solid object in motion around a star. Each planet has a color." He hesitated as if he were looking for the right words. He usually did that when he spoke to her, as if he thought she used a language different from his own. "It's a very distinctive color. Mercury is leaden, Venus silvery, Mars reddish, Jupiter white, and Saturn yellowish. They also have a characteristic brightness."

"I understand, Mr. Williams." Laurie tried to be polite, although she really wanted to tell him she'd enjoy it more listening like everyone else.

"The things that twinkle, you can't see them — sorry, Laurie, I didn't mean that. . . ."

"It's okay, Mr. Williams." She wished she could tell him she saw them in her way just the way he saw them in his or Betsy in hers, but Mr. Williams was a teacher. You just didn't have a conversation like that with a teacher.

"Well, they're probably not planets because planets don't twinkle. Know what I mean?"

"Sure, Mr. Williams. I know what you mean."

"The planets shine by light reflected from the sun, and on most clear nights, you can see one or more of them. I mean, they can be seen by anyone looking."

He shifted around for the right words. Laurie had another conversation playing around in her head while he spoke.

"Mr. Williams," she wanted to say, "don't worry about the words so much. I never think about them. I use *see* and *look* all the time."

"Mr. Williams, you sure are boring me."

"Mr. Williams, I'm blind. I'm not stupid."

"Mr. Williams, why don't you call up Mr. Stevens and let him tell you how great we got along because he didn't bother me about anything, and he minded his own business and I minded mine. He gave me my tests in braille because he knew braille, and if you really want to be able to do something for me, you can. Just plan ahead and get my work to Ms. Allen so she can have it transcribed into braille." That was the conversation playing around in her head all during the biology test and again today. It kept her from enjoying the planetarium and all it had to offer.

"The earth is the third of the known planets," Mr. Williams continued. "Mercury, Venus, Earth, Mars, Jupiter, Saturn, Uranus, Neptune, and Pluto. The first six were known to ancients; the remaining three were discovered in modern times."

"Boy, you sure are getting a private lesson today," Betsy whispered in her other ear. "Want some suckers?"

"Sure." Laurie grabbed one from Betsy's hand, but didn't put it in her mouth. She didn't feel like sucking on it next to Mr. Williams. She knew it wouldn't taste as good.

"The North Star is the really bright one. The ancient Egyptians thought it pointed the way to the realm of perpetual life."

Just then someone yelled "ouch" from the seats in front of them. Soon after, there was another "ouch."

"Mr. Williams, someone is shooting rubber bands at us," a girl complained.

"I'd better go see what's going on. Betsy, get me if Laurie needs anything," Mr. Williams instructed.

Laurie wanted to thank the rubber-band shooter, whoever it was. The disturbance in front kept Mr. Williams busy for the rest of the program and Laurie contentedly listening to the voice in her earphones.

By the time they got back to the school, though, Laurie was as nervous as Mr. Williams. He kept counting everyone to make sure they all were there, and when he was finished, he'd count them again.

"Betsy, stay with Laurie," he reminded her.

"Boy, he sure is hyper," Betsy said as they waited for the bus to go home. "He was sweating, and it isn't even warm out."

There was just enough time for Laurie to go home as she usually did and change her clothes before she went to work. But when she rushed into the kitchen, she found a note waiting for her

62

on the kitchen table where family members usually left their messages.

Don't go in to work today. Will talk to
you when we get home. Love, Mom and
Dad.

Laurie's curiosity wouldn't let her wait. Her first thought was that something had happened to George or to the shop. But when she called, he told her something she hadn't expected.

"Your mother called," he said. "She thought you were working too much and that this job was interfering with your schoolwork. I think she might be right, Laurie. I don't want you to do poorly in your classes. Not when you're planning to go to college some day."

"It was just one test I failed," Laurie protested. "I'll do better next time." But in a way she was relieved. Working less at George's meant taking fewer orders from George and listening less to George.

"I'm sure you'll do better next time," George agreed. "But let's stick to an hour or two Saturday mornings. That will help me out and make your parents feel better."

Jessie pushed the ball into Laurie's hands after she hung up the telephone. Saturday mornings wouldn't bring enough money for anything, Laurie thought, as she threw the ball for Jessie to catch. It was when she heard Jessie run for the ball that she felt guilty for not trying harder to keep the hours at George's bicycle shop. Jessie was playing her favorite game, and that meant the medicine was working.

"If Mr. Stevens doesn't get well soon and come back, I'll never pass another test in biology class," Laurie confided to Jessie when she returned the ball. "And then maybe Mom and Dad won't let me work at all."

Later that night, she and Jessie sat at the window staring up at the sky. Laurie knew so much more about the sky tonight than she had known the night before. The man talking in the earphones had explained that the stars were yellowish white and she knew now there was a Big Dipper up there, and a Little Dipper, and it looked like one of the ladles her mother used for serving soup, and that there were millions of stars. It was a very busy sky, so quiet when it wanted to be, so noisy with heavy rains pouring down and thunder tumbling across it and soft snow being dumped from it.

"I have so much to tell you about the sky," Laurie told Jessie when they finally snuggled beneath the blankets. But she was too tired, and decided it would wait until tomorrow.

7

They hadn't been on the beach together for a long time. Laurie had been afraid to take Jessie down there because it was harder for her to walk on the sand. But lately, during the past weeks, each day she seemed stronger. There were socks missing every day now, and yesterday Jessie had brought her ball over so many times that Laurie actually had told her, "No more, Jessie. Not until tomorrow."

Jessie loved the beach better than anything. Laurie could feel her tug at the leash as the sound of the ocean waves slapping against the jetties grew nearer. The seagulls flapped their wings overhead as if they were calling to them, leading the way to the sand.

"We'll just stay a little while, Jessie. We don't want to overdo it the first day. You can sniff all the seashells if you want."

Laurie's cane touched the steps that led to the

beach and tapped each of them as she walked down. She felt the afternoon sun bake against her skin as Jessie and she reached the soft sand. Laurie slipped off her socks and shoes, even though it was the beginning of November and much cooler than a summer day. But she never could walk the beach wearing her shoes and socks. She didn't miss the usual tourists' laughter or radios playing. There was just the sweet sound of the ocean, as if it knew it had everything to itself now.

"I'm going to make you a sand castle," Laurie told Jessie. She sat down in the sand and pulled Jessie with her. "It's going to be a special kingdom, where everybody likes everyone else, and nobody has arthritis and there are no Josephines. In fact, the first law will be that anybody mean can't come in. Only the kind people will be allowed to live in our kingdom. And being blind will be very respectable, like George says." She was thinking of Mr. Williams now. Maybe George was thinking of people like Mr. Williams, too, when he put up all the signs on his desk. The new one yesterday said BLIND IS COOL.

Even though the beach got deserted and damp and the wind much stronger, sending bits of sand stinging against her face, Laurie liked this time of year best of all. She felt the ocean must feel the same way, that it wanted privacy for a while, that it was tired of the summer crowds and all the garbage thrown around the beach and into the ocean waters by people who didn't care.

Laurie dug the hole deeper in front of her and piled the sand next to it. She could hear Jessie panting and digging with her, just like the old days when she was a puppy. While the mound in front of Laurie got taller, Jessie's hole got deeper. She wagged her tail each time Laurie's hand petted her.

"Good girl, Jessie. But just remember, before we leave, we've got to fill up these holes or somebody walking will fall into them and break an ankle."

The castle beneath Laurie's fingers grew taller and wider. She designed moats through which the ocean could send small streams each time the tide brought it closer to her. There were roads circling the kingdom and some doors outlined with her fingers and a few bridges that Laurie built with wet sand.

"We'll call it the Kingdom of Kindness," Laurie said aloud.

She was busy with a border circling the entire kingdom when Jessie growled.

"What's wrong, Jessie?" Laurie asked. "You angry at the seagulls?"

She put the finishing touches to the border, then touched the castle again to see if there was anything more needed before it was complete. Her hands moved toward the center but found nothing. The point at the top was gone. The bridges weren't there. She felt around, where all of it had been. In its place, she found lumps of sand scattered. Jessie's low growl persisted.

Then Laurie heard the familiar giggle.

"Did your Kingdom of Kindness fall down?" Josephine asked.

"I bet not without your help," Laurie answered.

"Don't get so touchy, Laurie. You sure can't take a joke, can you?"

"I don't think you're funny," Laurie told her as she got up. She reached toward the place where she had put her cane, but just like the castle, it had vanished.

"Give me my cane," she shouted at Josephine. She didn't mind losing the castle, but the cane was another matter. Especially on the beach. It was like an extension of her body, like an arm, and Laurie felt someone had just cut it off. She tried another tack.

"Look, I can't get home without it," she said.

"Oh, poor Laurie. Well, I guess you'll just have to stand there and be very nice to me so you can get your cane back."

Jessie knew something was going on that wasn't good for either of them. Her growl grew deeper. Laurie held on tightly to Jessie's leash.

"How about pretty please, Josephine. You can

say that, Laurie, can't you? Pretty please, Josephine, give me my cane back."

"Jessie, home," Laurie said instead. Whenever they finished their walks, Laurie would tell Jessie that and Jessie always knew which way to walk, wherever they were. But this time she felt Jessie pull the leash down.

"That dumb dog looks too old and tired to go anywhere." Josephine laughed. "He's just lying on the sand."

"Come on, Jessie. It's time for your bone," Laurie coaxed, but she felt no action on the other side of the leash. Whatever Jessie was thinking, she just didn't have the energy to go anywhere.

Laurie heard the keys jangle first, then Johnny Hayes's familiar voice.

"Give her back that cane, Josephine."

"I was going to give it back to her," Josephine answered. "Don't get so excited. It's just a dumb old cane anyway. I sure don't want it." Josephine was much farther away when she yelled, "That's just a dumb old cane."

"Here, Laurie," Johnny said. The white cane was placed in her hand. "I was running on the boardwalk when I saw that jerk Josephine heading your way." Laurie noticed his voice was low today. "That sure is a nice dog you've got there."

"Thanks," Laurie answered. She wondered if Betsy was right. Maybe Johnny Hayes *was* hanging around her, even when she didn't know it. This was the second time he had just popped up from nowhere.

"She's lying there as if she doesn't want to get up. And panting awfully hard."

"She does that when she gets excited. I guess the beach walking got her tired. She has arthritis." Laurie tugged the leash again, but Jessie didn't move.

"Does she bite?" Johnny asked.

"Not Jessie. She never bit anyone in her life. I don't even think she has enough teeth left if she wanted to."

"I'll carry her," Johnny offered.

Laurie figured Johnny Hayes had to be very strong to lift Jessie the way he did and carry her the four long blocks home, but he did just that.

"I wish I had a dog," he said on the way.

"Why don't you?" she asked.

"Because there's nobody home to take care of it. My mom said it wouldn't be fair, leaving it home alone all day. She wouldn't have the time, and I'm on the wrestling team after school. That's why I was running. The coach said it's good for me."

"Your mom's right about leaving a dog alone," Laurie told him. "I come home right after school to walk Jessie, and she really complains if the family goes out for the day. She stands there at the door looking so sad, and she's waiting right by the window when we come back. She sits on the couch looking out. We try to take her with us whenever we can."

"Good dog, Jess." Johnny laughed. "She's licking my face. I think she likes me."

"Jessie doesn't like just anybody. She sure didn't like Josephine."

She and Johnny had spent the four blocks talking. She couldn't wait to tell Betsy that it had been easy, and they didn't even talk about baseball.

"I live here," Laurie told him when they reached the middle of the fourth block.

Johnny put Jessie down and handed Laurie the leash. "Maybe I could visit Jessie sometimes," he said.

"Sure," Laurie answered. "Jessie loves visitors."

Laurie felt Jessie's tail wag against her leg as she politely showed her appreciation for the ride home. She didn't hear the keys jangle as she had all the way home. He was still standing there next to her, as if he had something else to say.

"How do you know?" Johnny finally asked.

"How do I know what?" Laurie was puzzled.

"How do you know it's your house?" Johnny asked.

"How do you know when you get to your house?" Laurie asked him back.

71

"Because my house is brown and it's got a white door and it's my house," he said.

"Well, my house is pale green and it's got a white door, too, and it's my house," Laurie told him. "And it also has a chip in the cement in front of it and a big maple tree at the curb."

She left him there after another thank-you to think about it. As soon as she got into the house, she hung up her cane on the hat rack, alongside the hats and umbrellas. There was no need for her to use it in the house. It was different on the beach, or whenever she walked outside her home.

There were two pieces of paper waiting for her when she checked the kitchen table. One was an envelope from her grandmother. The other was a note from her mother: "We went shopping for food. It would help if you'd start the salad and set the table when you get home."

Laurie changed her clothes, which were covered with sand, and then went down to the kitchen. She took the lettuce from the refrigerator, and the tomatoes and some carrots and cucumbers. There were also some string beans and broccoli, and some onions on the bottom shelf. She washed everything and then began to cut the vegetables on the wooden board that pulled out from the sink.

The telephone ringing interrupted her concentration.

"Hello, Laurie. This is Dr. Nick's office," the receptionist said. "Are your parents home?"

"No," Laurie answered. "But they'll be home soon."

"Well, perhaps you can give them a message. Just tell them we got their note and it's no problem. They can pay off Jessie's bill a little at a time. The doctor understands, okay?"

"Okay," Laurie answered.

But it wasn't really okay. There obviously wasn't enough money each month in the household budget that her father worked on each Friday night. Laurie stood by the telephone for a long time, wondering how she could bring in more money to help out with the bills. Two hours a week at George's bicycle shop was not enough, and her parents would certainly not agree to let her work more. Especially since her marks were not as high as they had been with Mr. Stevens.

She wished her grandmother were sitting right next to her in the room when she finally sat down to read her letter. She needed to put her arms around her, tonight especially, when there seemed to be so many questions without answers.

Dear Laurie Sweetcake:
    Don't worry so much about Jessie and if she has a good day or a bad day. When

you get old, you don't have a string of good days in a row, but you sure can have a string of bad days. You get used to that, though, and you do what you can on the good days. I just hate when people keep asking me how I feel because I don't think that's such interesting news, and what does it matter anyway how I feel? What matters is how I think and what I do to make the day better. So stop letting Jessie know that you're staring at her all the time wondering if it's a good day or a bad one.

We had a big garage sale at the nursing home yesterday. I sold off a lot of junk and then I bought even more junk. At least that's what Margaret, my roommate, said. But don't you think she is the one watering the plant I bought and talking to it each morning? I'm sending you a bottle of marbles, not the phony colored plastic ones, but the old glass ones, so take care of them and don't give them away. I kept a bottle for myself, though I'm sure nobody wants to play games here. Though you never can tell about Margaret.

Kiss Jessie and your parents for me and tell Katherine I think she must have broken her fingers at college because she never writes.

Love, Grandmom

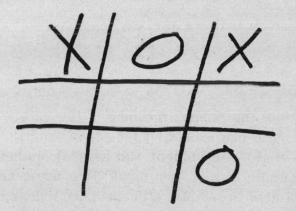

"Thank you, Grandmom," Laurie said as she ran up the stairs to her bedroom. "You've just given me the answer."

8

It was the Sunday morning of the garage sale Laurie had organized for Jessie, and the sky was bright with sunlight. But Laurie's mother had something else on her mind. "We made an appointment to see Mr. Williams next Friday," she told Laurie. "We've got to see if we can do something about these marks you're getting in his class. And truthfully, Laurie, you're not doing so well this year in any other class."

Laurie couldn't argue with her mother about that. Wondering about Mr. Williams and why he was doing all the things he was doing made her wonder about all the other teachers. Even though they all gave her tests in braille, she began to notice little things, like how they didn't talk to her the way they talked to everybody else in class. She began to notice the way they talked to her, and the way they sometimes forgot to tell her what they wrote on the blackboard, and sometimes even the way they joked with everybody else. She had never thought about things like that before, but Mr. Williams treated her differently than anyone else she had known. And now she was beginning to think she was different.

"Mr. Williams seems very nice," her mother continued. "He said he was about to call us because he thought you needed some help in biology."

He was right about that. She did need help. But not with the work. She needed help with the teacher. Yet she couldn't tell her mother that. She didn't want her running up to school like Betsy's mother, who was still fighting for the left-handed desks and whom Betsy was trying to avoid every time her mother came to school. She wanted to take care of it herself. She felt you couldn't force somebody to understand something like this. You had to show them.

"I also told George that you wouldn't be in next weekend. I know you were planning to go to work but until we find out what's going on with these marks, Dad and I think it better that you not work at all."

Not work at all. The words took the hope right out of Laurie's garage sale. No matter what she made today, it wouldn't make up for the money George paid her.

"We've got to set up the tables in the driveway," Betsy told her when she arrived exactly at the time she'd said she would. "This is a real important day so I made up my mind to be here on time. We've got to put all the piles of clothes on one table, and the toys on the other." Betsy was an excellent organizer.

"I went into the attic with my mom last night and we found so many things I don't need anymore," Laurie said as she helped Betsy open the card table. "I'm going to sell all my old games and the clothes that don't fit me anymore. Katherine even told me where to look in the attic to find some of her old stuff. And my dad put in all his old golf clubs and balls because he bowls now. And he says if he ever wants to golf again and we have more money, he'll buy new ones."

That's all her dad worried about lately. Money. Even last night, she heard, through the thin walls of their bedroom, her parents talking about it.

"You work and work," her mother said, "and what good does it do? We still don't have enough money at the end of the week. I don't know where it goes."

Her father had answered, "It gets pretty discouraging, honey. I want to buy things for you and the girls and I want to do things. I was thinking of taking on a second job."

But Laurie's mother had turned down that idea. "And then what? Get sick from overwork?" she had said. "We'll make do with what we have and make the best of it. As long as you're in good health, that's being rich."

Laurie's father had always called her mother an optimist, and Laurie guessed that's what he meant.

"I brought some stuff, too," Betsy said. "I didn't need these coloring books and crayons any more. I wanted to do something for Jessie, also."

The sale was listed in the classified section of the newspaper for 12:00 to 4:00 Sunday afternoon.

"Something for everyone," Laurie had advertised. "Lots of treasures."

"What do you think we should ask for the clothes?" Betsy asked. She held some stickers that were to be placed on a pile in front of her.

"I talked to my grandmom. She used to go to garage sales all the time with her friends. They even hold them at the nursing home. She says to price them fairly and low because people know they're used goods and not new, and if they had money, they'd go to the department stores and buy them new. It's important, Grandmom says, to sell everything you've got."

Some familiar keys jangled. "You can put these in," Johnny Hayes said. He handed Laurie three toy trucks and some plastic water pistols. "I don't really use them any more," he said. "Besides, Jessie will need plenty of medicine because she's going to live a long time, aren't you Jessie?" Then Johnny helped set up a sign in front of a table. It read, ALL MONEY FROM THIS SALE WILL GO TO JESSIE'S MEDICINE FUND.

Laurie realized how close Johnny had become to Jessie. Johnny stopped over a couple of times a week since he had carried Jessie home that day. Sometimes he played with Jessie in the living room. Sometimes he brought her a treat, like a ball one day and a bone another. Usually, during Jessie's play time, Laurie and Johnny would talk. They did more talking than Laurie ever remembered doing with anybody else, and it was easier, too. She never had to think about what they were going to talk about next. In fact, there were always more things she thought of to say right after he left, and it must have been the same with Johnny because sometimes he'd call at night after dinner to tell her something, even though he had just been there.

Laurie put Johnny in charge of the toy table. She and Betsy were behind the clothes table, and Laurie's mother had a belt around her waist and was in charge of making change and taking money. Laurie's dad helped put things into packages if anyone needed it. People began arriving even before 12:00.

"Oh, what lovely clothes," one woman said. She put a pile in front of Laurie.

"One dollar," Laurie said, feeling the stack.

"That's fine," the woman answered. "And I'll take some of these coloring books and crayons."

"Would you take any less for this tray?" a man bargained. "It's marked two dollars."

Betsy's mother had contributed the tray. "One-fifty," Laurie's mother bargained back.

Laurie felt bits of her past disappear as the tables emptied. Part of the little girl in her left with each sale. She felt almost as if she were growing up as the afternoon ended.

Later, Betsy and Johnny and Laurie and her parents sat in the kitchen and counted up all the money.

"Eighty dollars," her father said, as if he couldn't believe it. "I can't believe so many people care about Jessie and what happens to her." Laurie had never heard her father cry, but for a few moments she thought he was about to. He wasn't a man who was used to showing his feelings. As Laurie sat there hearing the emotion in his voice, she realized he cared more about Jessie than he had let anyone know.

Laurie knew it was a nice sum of money, enough for more than two months of Jessie's medicine, but then what? Where would the money come from next time? She had used up just about everything she could sell in this garage sale.

But as worried as Laurie was about paying for Jessie's medication, the meeting between her mother and Mr. Williams coming up on Friday monopolized her thoughts. She thought about it all Monday, through all her classes, and by Tuesday she could think of nothing else. It was as if she weren't even sitting behind the desk in class.

Maybe it was just as well, because sometimes lately, she felt nobody knew she was even there. At Baker, everybody had joked with her. Everybody liked her. Everybody knew her.

But toward the middle of the week, the frown that had been with her all through the classes turned into a smile. She knew just what to do to solve one of her problems: straightening out Mr. Williams.

"Want to go roller-skating?" she asked Johnny when he came over to visit Jessie on Wednesday. She trusted him just as much now as she trusted Betsy.

"I thought you didn't like roller-skating," he said. Johnny kindly did not mention her roller-skating fall and the two bruised knees.

"I don't. But I've got to learn. All you have to do is skate in front of me and just yell 'bump' if you see one coming." She didn't tell him his jangling keys would help her keep track of where he was going.

"I'll go get my skates," Johnny said. While he went home, Laurie took hers from the closet.

"Bump, bump, bump," Johnny yelled as they skated down the sidewalk. The white cane found the bumps gradually and by the second hour, the cane found them even before Johnny did.

"You sure must like to roller-skate," Johnny said on Thursday, after they had roller-skated all afternoon after school. They stopped only when it got dark and Johnny was afraid that he wouldn't see the bumps anymore. But by that time, Laurie could find them herself. "Don't you want to walk on the boardwalk instead? Or maybe watch some television?"

They had done that, too, after school, with Jessie of course — watched TV while Johnny answered her questions, if there were any, about what was happening on the screen.

"What have you got there?" her mother asked as Laurie picked up a paper bag on Friday morning.

"Just some junk I have to take to school," Laurie answered in a rush. "Got to go." She hurried out the door, unwilling to be questioned any more.

"You're not really going to do it, are you?" Betsy asked later, in the schoolyard. "I mean, you're not really serious, are you?"

"I sure am," Laurie answered. "Just watch me." She strapped the roller skates on her shoes, then tightened them with her key. "I'll meet you inside," she told Betsy. It was one of the few times she was glad she didn't see the expression on Betsy's face. Then she took the cane and roller-skated into school. She roller-skated down the hallway amidst laughter and some shouts of encouragement.

"Way to go, Laurie," someone yelled.

She didn't go too fast because she didn't want

to hurt anybody in her way. Laurie knew Mr. Williams always waited in the hallway in the morning, in front of his homeroom classroom, until the bell rang. She knew when she reached it and she knew when he saw her.

"Laurie! Be careful! You're not allowed to roller-skate in the hall," he shouted.

Laurie circled in front of him. Twice.

"You're going to hurt yourself," he warned. She heard him running after her, and then the chase was on. Laurie moved her skates faster, the cane sweeping back and forth. The hall got quiet, except for feet scurrying off to the side of the hall. Usually when there was a crowd walking around her, Laurie would hold the white cane close to her side so that she wouldn't hit anybody with it. Today she wanted everyone to scatter out of her way.

"Come back here," Mr. Williams called. "That's against the rules."

Laurie smiled. It had worked. For once, he had forgotten that she was blind. All that he remembered was that she was a student at Bradley breaking the rules.

"I'm going to have to report you," he told her later as they went down to the front office. He was having trouble keeping up with her since she still had on the roller skates.

"I understand, Mr. Williams," she said.

"I don't know what got into you today," Mr.

Williams said. "Now take those things off, will you?"

Laurie hoped that when he thought about it, he would figure it out. If not, her parents sure would explain things to him after school today, when they met with him and found out how she was being given her tests. They were smart enough to put it all together. They were sure to be on her side.

Later, after the principal had explained to Laurie how dangerous it could have been for her and others if she had fallen with the roller skates, and after she was given a warning that the next time there would be more than just a warning, and after everyone in the hall had congratulated her on her great arrival at school, Laurie placed the roller skates in her locker.

Mr. Williams wasn't the only one who learned something today, Laurie realized, as she walked toward her next class. The kids at school had been taught something about Laurie, too. She was just like them. She could break the rules, sometimes, when necessary.

9

Not even the anticipation of going to the circus could wipe away Laurie's disappointing week. It just shows you how wrong you can be about something, Laurie thought, as she and Betsy walked out of the house. Laurie had just changed the tip for her traveling cane to replace the one that had worn out.

Now Betsy and she were ready to walk the few blocks to the circus. But Laurie could not chase the shadows that followed her today. She thought everything would be straightened out at school by now, but instead, things were more mixed up than ever. Now everybody was mad at her. After their meeting with Mr. Williams, her parents came back and grounded Laurie for one week.

"You had no business roller-skating through that hall," they said, "and you should have told us right away what was going on with those tests. We thought you trusted us enough to tell us things like that, and we thought we could trust you."

As if that weren't bad enough, Mr. Williams wasn't too happy about any of it. Even though he was giving her tests in braille that were made up by Ms. Allen and even though he didn't walk her to the bus anymore, he seemed even more ill at ease when he was around her. Before, at least he had been friendly. Now he was just very quiet. Maybe it was because her parents had gone to the principal and complained about the whole thing.

Laurie didn't say much as she and Betsy continued their walk to the circus. Her mind was too busy trying to figure out why nothing had turned out the way she thought it would. Even George had to get his opinion in. Yesterday, when Betsy got a flat and they went over to George's to get a new tire because George guaranteed all his bicycles for six months, flat tires and all, George sure wasn't on her side when he found out about the situation between Laurie and her teacher. George always had a way of finding out things even when Laurie had made up her mind not to tell him.

"Don't blame everything on Mr. Williams," he told her, while he changed Betsy's tire. "There's nothing wrong with your mouth. You could have asked him not to walk you to the bus and you could have explained things to him. After all, how are you going to educate people if you walk around sulking and not telling them what you think? You've got to tell people what you can do and what you need help in doing and what you'd like to learn, just like everybody else in this world. They're not mind readers, you know. And if that didn't work, you should have told your parents. So stop complaining. Not everybody has to like you, and not everybody has to know what you like. That goes for the sighted and the blind." And then, as if he thought she still didn't understand, he announced loud enough so that everyone in the store heard, "Being blind doesn't entitle you to a free ride through life."

"I thought you'd feel great about going to the circus," Betsy said. "You haven't said a word for three blocks."

"I just don't feel like talking today."

"You always feel like talking."

"No, I don't. Not always."

"Always."

"I should know if I don't always feel like talking."

"Well, so should I, because I'm the one you're usually talking to."

"No, you're not. I talk to Johnny Hayes most every day."

"Well, I talk to Ellen and Barbara, and last week Jasper Hoffman called me."

"What are we fighting about?" Laurie asked on the fourth block.

"I don't know. You started it."

"I started it? I didn't say anything."

Luckily they had reached the circus admission booth by that time.

"That's two dollars," said the lady at the front booth.

Laurie took the money from her pocketbook.

"There's no charge for the blind girl," the woman said to Betsy.

"Boy, you're lucky," Betsy said, handing Laurie back her money. "You get in free today."

"I heard her," Laurie snapped. There was something about getting into the circus for nothing that went up her back, like a piece of chalk screeching on a blackboard. Maybe George was right, she thought as she stood there, the money in her hand feeling heavier by the minute. Maybe you had to tell someone what you thought and why you thought it, or they'd never know.

"Here's my money," Laurie said, after going back to the booth. "There's no reason you should let me go in for nothing."

"But honey . . ." the woman started to say. Laurie felt much better after she left her money at the booth and received her ticket to go inside.

"And you said you're not in a bad mood today," Betsy remarked, as they walked over the gravel parking lot where the circus was making its home for the week.

"There's just nothing special about being blind," Laurie explained to Betsy, sounding more like George as she spoke. Her tone softened. She hated taking out her bad moods on her best friend. "Let's go find the elephants," she said.

Laurie liked to read about circuses, and especially about elephants, when she went to the library.

"I want to ride an elephant," she told Betsy. "There's a wildlife reserve in southern India," she continued as the sounds of the circus lightened her mood. "Elephants are great parents. They treat their young so well and they have relatives all over the place, cousins and uncles and aunts. And even though they're big, they seem so gentle. I always wanted to touch one of their long trunks."

Someone handed Laurie a balloon and tickled her under the chin.

"He's a clown," Betsy told her. "He's got a big red nose like a ball, and all kinds of paints on his face and a tall checkered hat and large white flopping shoes and his pants are so big, they look like they could have someone else in there with him. He's carrying one, two, three, four, five, six, seven, eight, nine, ten," Betsy counted, "eleven balloons."

It didn't take long to find the elephants.

"How big is he?" Laurie asked, when Betsy yelled that there was one standing right in front of them.

"Real big," she answered.

"How big do you mean by real big?"

"Like thousands of pounds piled up on top of each other."

While they were discussing it, a woman asked, "Want to take a ride, little girl? Only fifty cents to ride on Big Bertha."

"You've got to climb up the steps on the side of the elephant and there's a chair on top of her," Betsy explained. "Somebody straps you into the chair so you won't fall off."

"Let's do it," Laurie said.

"There's only one seat," Betsy told her. "I'm not sure I want to go on alone."

"Well, I do." Laurie gave the woman the money and with the guidance of her cane and some instructions from the woman and Betsy, she made her way close enough to the elephant to feel his trunk sweep against her leg. Her hands trailed up the trunk as far as they could go as Laurie stretched to reach as much of Bertha as she could.

"I don't know about this," the woman organizing the ride said. "I don't want you hurting yourself."

"Don't worry," Laurie reassured her, remembering George's advice. "I know plenty about elephants. I read about them all the time."

Much to Laurie's surprise, when the woman shouted, "Kneel," the elephant obeyed. She felt the trunk slide down and rest on the ground. Carefully, Laurie climbed up the steps. Even though the elephant was kneeling, she got a good idea of how big "big" was when she finally reached the chair. She stroked Bertha's leathery skin while she was strapped into the chair by the woman who had followed her up the steps.

"Don't be afraid," the woman cautioned. "Bertha is very gentle."

The ride was a bumpy one and much too short for Laurie, who pretended she was in southern India on one of those reserves, leading an elephant herd to food and water.

"Everybody was staring at you and Bertha," Betsy told her, after the ride was finished and Laurie had said her good-byes to Bertha. Laurie usually didn't enjoy being stared at. She could feel people staring sometimes when she walked into a room. That kind of staring bothered her. This kind didn't. Bertha probably didn't mind it either.

There was plenty of cotton candy to eat as they walked around the circus and enjoyed the music playing and the sounds of animals and the smells of hay and food. They sat through the trapeze act and the tightrope walkers'.

"They always look like they're going to fall," Betsy told her. "They're walking across a rope with their arms held out, balancing themselves, and there's a big net underneath just in case. It's really scary."

Laurie could tell it was by the loud roll of the

drums and the screams of the people in the audience.

When they stood in front of the lions' cage listening to them roar and slap their bodies against the walls as they circled it, Betsy told her, "There's a man inside there with them. He's got a whip and he keeps cracking it in front of the lions to keep them back."

Laurie pictured the lions she had read about in the braille books. The man inside the cage with them must be brave and very certain that he had control of the animals pacing around him.

"You should have taken a ride on the elephant," Laurie told Betsy hours later, when they stood in front of Betsy's house. "It was like being on top of the world."

Laurie had forgotten everything else in her life at the circus, and riding Bertha was all she could talk about all the way home. But once she opened the front door to her house, the problems there returned.

There was a letter from Grandmom waiting for Laurie on the kitchen table, as usual. The letters were coming more frequently lately, since Jessie had been sick. It was as if Grandmom were living through everything with Laurie, as if she had a room right down their hall or lived down the block. Letters could make you feel that close to someone, Laurie thought.

Dear Laurie,

I thought about nothing else these last weeks but Jessie. I am quite aware that Jessie is a dog and that I am a human being, but you cannot believe how similar our problems are. I too spend much of my time napping, and I too find it difficult to get around, and yes, it costs me plenty of money to keep up this medicine for all the parts of my body. It seems I need a pill to get everything working that used to work quite well without anything. Getting old is not an easy matter. People sometimes forget you exist, or maybe they think something happened to your mind. But then again, I guess growing up isn't easy either. Especially when you have to face a Josephine.

I was putting myself in Jessie's place. I guess I know I wouldn't want to go on living if I couldn't eat and couldn't drink and couldn't think. I guess those are the three couldn'ts that would make me welcome ending something here and beginning it elsewhere. You know there should be nothing sad about a new beginning. But maybe it's the same with Jessie. Maybe she'll just show everyone when she's had enough. She probably won't want to eat and won't want to drink and won't want to do anything. She'll be so miserable that she'll send the message out so you understand that she doesn't want to be cranked up and pushed around with needles and pills any more. But remember, it's not just an ending, it's also a beginning.

But the way you tell me she's acting, I don't think you have to worry about that right now. I just wanted you to realize that someday you're going to have to let go when Jessie wants you to. If you love her, you'll do that for her. But letting go doesn't mean you'll lose her. Memories remain forever, and that's where I want to be some day for you, also. Forever in your memories.

But Jessie and I both are still kicking and fussing and we're not going anywhere this minute. I am sending in a separate package half a dozen grapefruit, and a bag of sunflower seeds. Also, a package of chocolates.

I know your mother is trying to keep everybody on this health-food diet, but I don't think anybody ever grew up without some chocolate and ice cream and taffy. My mother used to say, "Too much of anything isn't good." So I guess that applies to all that good tasteless stuff your mother enjoys.

Now Sweetcake, stay well. When I sent you the roller skates, I didn't dream you would be so creative. Your parents sure went into a tizzy on that one.

I love you . . .
                    Your turn,
                              Grandmom

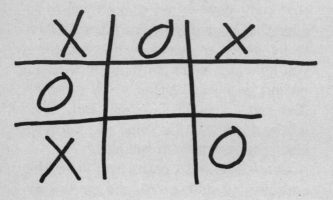

Laurie reread the letter over and over, and each time she did, it kept making her feel better. About everything.

10

It wasn't the best day for Jessie to go walking. The cold winter winds didn't do her arthritis any good, but today Jessie kept going to the front door and scratching at it. When Jessie made up her mind to do something, nothing much could change it. Though she was content to walk slowly, Jessie insisted on sniffing just about every tree trunk and garbage can that stood on the curb.

"You're doing just fine," Laurie said as they walked down the street. She wished she were as certain about her father and how he was doing. Today there was a fresh bottle of arthritis pills next to Jessie's Milk-Bone jar. And last week there had been another bill on the kitchen table from the veterinarian.

It seemed they were on a road without an end. Every time her dad asked how Jessie was feeling, Laurie felt he was waiting for something, like being released from a promise. After he paid the bills each month, he'd sit there for a long time, as if he were thinking, as if thinking would make the bills go away.

Suddenly, Laurie felt the leash tighten. Jessie pulled at it. Laurie heard her growl, the kind of growl that was a sign of danger. It was more of a snarl. If someone got too near her dinner dish and she was especially hungry, or if she had one of those good soup bones Betsy often brought over, Jessie would warn everybody with that growl.

This time it continued, getting stronger, and so did the pull at the other end of the leash.

"What is it, Jessie?" Laurie asked. "What's wrong, girl? Take it easy."

Another, louder bark joined Jessie's. It was an angry barking, urgent, vicious, mixed in with Jessie's protests. Now the leash in Laurie's hand was yanked from it as the two dogs, Jessie and another, howled their warnings at each other.

"Jessie, let's go. Come on. We've got to get home," Laurie begged. She moved the white cane around, trying to find the leash, but Jessie was not in front of her anymore. Instead she heard a thrashing about, two bodies slapping against one another several feet up the street.

"Jessie, come here!" she screamed, but Jessie either couldn't or didn't want to. "Could someone help me," Laurie shouted. She listened for a passerby, but the streets sounded unusually empty.

The block was silent except for the two dogs

and the angry sounds from both of them. Laurie could only imagine the size of the other dog and what it was doing to Jessie. The picture in her mind drove her to call for help even louder.

Was it five minutes, or five seconds? Laurie couldn't judge, but it seemed forever before she heard the other dog scurry away and a whimpering sound from Jessie, closer to her.

Laurie bent down and caught the leash that was now in front of her feet. She touched Jessie's body, but even beneath her light touch, Jessie whimpered.

"You're bleeding, Jessie," she sobbed, as moisture clung to her hand.

Footsteps hurried toward her.

"Can I help?" a woman asked. "I saw that fight from down the block. That dog was twice the size of yours. I don't know how your beagle fought him off."

"Please go to my home . . . 305 Archer Street, right around the corner. Tell my parents I need them. My dog's been hurt."

She waited, comforting Jessie, who lay flat on the ground near her feet, panting heavily.

"It's okay, Jessie," she said. "You're going to be fine." But even as she tried to reassure her friend, she wondered what a battle like this could do to such an old and frail body.

When her father got there, Laurie quickly told him what happened.

"I can't get her to stand," she said. "And she's bleeding, Dad."

"No, she's not, honey. That's sweat you feel. She's just winded. Let's take her over to Dr. Nick's right away. She's probably just in shock. She really doesn't look too bad, honey," her father tried to reassure her.

Dr. Nick took them right into the examination room when they got there.

"How bad is it?" her dad asked anxiously. "The neighbor told me she got into quite a fight this time. The dog was twice her size. I don't know how she persevered."

"Well, she was fighting for her life," Dr. Nick said, "and probably for Laurie's safety, so she gave it everything she had." There was a long quiet period while they waited for the examination to be completed.

"Her heart is pumping, good and strong," Dr. Nick said. "She's got some bites over her body but they aren't deep, and with a little antibiotic they should heal. She did a good job of protecting herself."

"I guess you're not done living yet, are you, old dog?" her father asked. Laurie didn't expect to hear her father confide to the doctor, "To tell you the truth, Doc, I'm so attached to Jessie, it's hard to imagine our days without her."

Laurie was amazed at the emotion in her father's voice. She had never realized before how much he loved Jessie, too, and how much he must have been suffering.

"You're right about Jessie," Dr. Nick agreed. "She's still got that spark lit in her. She'll let you know when it goes out. I think she's got some good years left in her. Aside from the arthritis, she's got a strong healthy body. You've been taking good care of her."

"Well, she takes good care of all of us. And to tell you the truth, Doc, she keeps that spark lit in me." It was a surprise for Laurie to hear her father say that, and more. "These past months things haven't been too good on the job, but you know, when I come home, and Jessie's there not losing her spirit, not giving up, I think to myself, well, I guess I can't give up either. It's funny how things like that can become important to you."

Then Dr. Nick gave him some samples of antibiotics and Jessie a painkiller so that she could sleep peacefully for a few hours while the bruises subsided.

"Come on, old dog," Laurie's dad called later that night when Jessie got out of her basket. "How about some pistachio nuts?"

Jessie shelled hers while they watched television together. Somehow, hearing Jessie called "old dog" didn't bother Laurie as it once had. She understood her father better now. She realized that just because he didn't talk about the way he felt didn't mean those deep feelings weren't there.

The way her father said "old dog" tonight made it sound like a compliment, almost like it was some kind of honor to grow old.

The next morning, Grandmom Beatrice called before Laurie left for school.

"How you doing, Sweetcake?" Grandmom asked. She wasn't a telephone person, so Laurie knew it must be important.

"I'm fine, Grandmom. You want to talk to Mom?"

"No, honey. I want to talk to you. I've got a great idea."

"What about?" Laurie asked.

"Jessie, of course. You know all that stuff I send you, the candy and the taffy and those big pineapples. Well, I was thinking, for a while, until your father is certain about what's going on with this job, how about if I take the money I'd usually spend on all these odds and ends, and put it into the Jessie fund."

"The Jessie fund?" Laurie asked. "What kind of fund is that?"

"For her arthritis pills, of course, what else? You'd be surprised how those nickels and dimes could add up during the month. I bet I could pay half of it before you'd know it."

"Would you do that, Grandmom?" Laurie's voice showed her delight.

"Would you do it, Sweetcake, sacrifice the presents that you usually get? You know, birthdays

. . . holidays . . . I'm always getting you something, but I don't think I could manage that and the Jessie fund both. Understand?"

Laurie understood perfectly. The sacrifice was a small one compared to what she would gain. And if her marks went up, and she was sure they would now because things were changing, maybe not as much with Mr. Williams as they were inside herself, if those marks began to climb, maybe then she could go back to work at George's a couple of hours a week and add her own donations to the Jessie fund.

That day she couldn't wait to get to school. She had persuaded George to speak to her class. Everyone Laurie knew was always complaining that their bicycles had broken down. "You could come to school to talk to all our classes on bicycle repair and how to take care of your bicycle," she had told George. "And you could also tell them the way you told me about keeping their bicycles locked so they won't get stolen." George finally agreed, though he made it clear he would rather be fixing a bicycle than talking about it.

"This is Mr. Williams." Betsy introduced her teacher to George when he came into the classroom later that day. "And this is George Salvadore," she told the students.

Everybody in the class got very still while George spoke. There was something about George's voice that made you listen whether you wanted to or not. Today Laurie actually enjoyed hearing George share all the things he knew about bicycles.

Betsy nudged her. "He's got on the sweatshirt that says 'Braille Readers Are Cool.' "

George put everything into his program. He told everybody in class how he could tell if there was a hole in a tire and how they could tell too . . . by passing the tube over the side of his cheek and under his chin . . . and how then he could feel the air coming out. He showed them how he plugged a leak with a toothpick that marked the hole, and then how he put glue on the patch.

"When I want to fill a tire to the correct pressure, I just thump the rubber. The spikes give off a special vibration when the tires are properly inflated."

"He sure is smart," Johnny Hayes said, as he and Betsy and Laurie walked down the hall after class. "He took apart the whole bicycle and put it back together again. I can't do that and I could see everything."

Even Mr. Williams was impressed, Laurie thought, as she walked down the hallway alone after they left to go to their other classes.

"I really do a lot of bicycle riding," he told George after class. "Could you run through showing me how to find those leaks again?"

Of course George was glad to do that, and

Laurie felt Mr. Williams was going to learn more from George than just how to repair a bicycle.

"Are you going to bring all your friends to school to show us how to do things, Laurie?" Josephine taunted. The voice was in front of her. The white cane found Josephine's feet blocking the way.

"I can't go through you," Laurie warned Josephine. "Please get out of the way."

"I am out of the way," Josephine lied.

Laurie had run out of patience. She knew Josephine was not the type that she could reason with or persuade. She also knew Josephine would never like her, and Laurie realized that she no longer cared if she did. Because she didn't like Josephine.

WHACK!

"OUCH!"

WHACK! again.

"You hit my ankle with that dumb cane. You hit me on purpose," Josephine wailed.

Laurie smiled as the way cleared. Applause from her classmates followed her all the way down the school hallway.

About the Author

HARRIET MAY SAVITZ is the author of more than sixteen books for children and is co-founder of the Philadelphia Children's Reading Round Table. She was born in Newark, New Jersey, and now lives right near the beach in Bradley Beach, New Jersey. Ms. Savitz, with her late husband, Ephraim, has two grown children, Beth and Steven, and two grandchildren, Ryan and Jenny, who provide her with new stories every day.

Harriet May Savitz's Apple Paperbacks include *Swimmer*, *The Cats Nobody Wanted*, and *The Bullies and Me*. Ms. Savitz, a dedicated animal lover, lives with four cats, one dog, and two box turtles.